BOUND BY LOVE

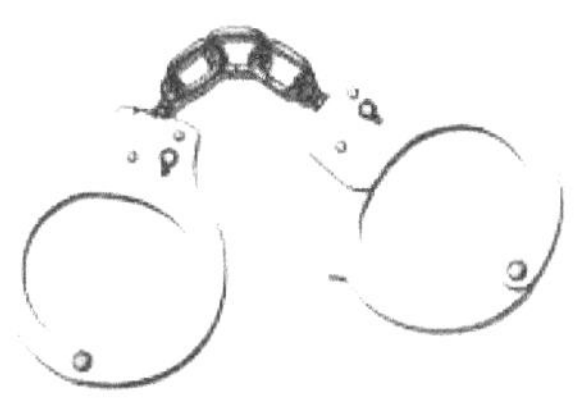

Susan Horsnell

USA Today Bestselling Author

Contents:

Author of Amazon No 1 Best Sellers in 2018:

Matt—Book 1 in The Carter Brothers Series

Clay—Book 3 in The Carter Brothers Series

Amazon No 1 Best Seller in February 2019

Andrew's Outback Love—Book 1 in The Outback Australia Series

Amazon No 1 Best Seller in July 2019

Ruby's Outback Love—Book 2 in The Outback Australia Series

Amazon No 1 Best Seller in May 2019

Eight Letters

Will—Book 2 in The Carter Brothers Series

Amazon Best Seller in April 2020

Cora: Bride of South Dakota

BOUND BY LOVE

This is a work of fiction. Similarities to real people, places, or events are entirely coincidental.

Written by Susan Horsnell

Edited: Redline Editing

Proofread: Leanne Rogers

Published by: Lipstick Publishing

ABN: 573-575-99847

Cover by Jocelyn from

https://www.facebook.com/groups/DexpressCovers/383132782574511

Warning

This book contains sexual content and language suitable only for those 18+

Disclaimer

This book is a work of fiction. Any resemblance to persons, living or dead, or places, events or locales is purely coincidental or historical. The characters are productions of the author's imagination and/or are used fictitiously.

This is a fictional story and although there may be some facts included, the author does not have personal knowledge of the law, the police or BDSM. It is created or embellished for the sake of the story.

Chapter One

Imogen glanced across the courtroom and noted Aaron seated in the public gallery. Muscles bunched under his shirt stretching it tight. Locks of his glossy black hair hung over his forehead and his piercing blue eyes locked with hers. Warmth pooled in her pussy; she found it difficult to concentrate knowing his hungry gaze was watching her every move.

Aaron curled his lips into a grin, he hadn't missed Imogen squirming uncomfortably when she had first noticed him in the gallery. His beautiful, tall, leggy brunette rose from her chair, turned her back and began fiddling with papers. He knew he was being unfair unsettling her in this way. This was an important trial for his Sub. It involved the Mayor's son and could make or break her brilliant career.

Imogen breathed deeply. She couldn't let her clients down by being distracted. She loved Sir dearly, but she would have to talk with him. She couldn't have him attending this trial and distracting her.

"Please rise for the Honourable Judge Dalton O'Malley," a voice from the front of the courtroom announced.

Imogen came to attention and when she dared to take a quick peek in the direction of the gallery, she noticed Aaron had left. She exhaled with relief.

Aaron strolled outside into the bright sunshine. He had done what he had come to do. His Sub needed to be kept informed of who was in charge at all times. He smiled to himself as he headed for his favorite café at Circular Quay.

He would enjoy a latté while he drank in the first warmth of summer and made plans for tonight.

He weaved his way down George Street, smiling at several women and girls as he went. He was well aware his physique attracted interest, but he had the only woman he wanted. Imogen was his whole life, he would never hurt her by straying.

He entered the café on the waterfront and was immediately shown to a table overlooking the harbor. The view was magnificent. The water sparkled in the sunlight and vessels of every shape, color and size floated in all directions. Aaron was content. He picked up the daily paper which had been placed down with his latté and began reading.

He would not pick Imogen up from the trial. He would meet her at home, he had something special in mind.

***

Imogen smiled as the Barrister stood and glanced her way. He was ready to begin the defense of his client.

Madison James, a 60-year-old closet drunk and a family friend of the young accused, could not be taken lightly. His knowledge of the law and fierce dedication to his clients was legendary and he was defending the Mayor's son on this occasion. Imogen knew she would have to stay alert.

Madison approached the young man. "Timothy, can you please tell the court where you were on the night of January 5 this year."

"Yes, Sir. I was in the Jailhouse Bar in Pitt Street. I left around midnight and went straight home. "The young man in the dock was clean shaven and dressed in a brown Armani suit. Imogen estimated his age at about twenty-five. His brown eyes were bright and confidence oozed from every pore of his body. She took an instant dislike to him.

"Who were you with?" Madison continued the questioning.

"I went there alone but spoke to a couple of people."

"Do you usually go alone?"

"No, but I didn't decide to go there until around 10pm and I knew that would be too late for my usual friends."

"Did you see the victim, Janet Linton, on the evening of January 5 this year?"

"No Sir. I did not. I hadn't seen Janet for more than a week."

Imogen listened as denial poured from the man's mouth. No, he hadn't seen her, no, he didn't go anywhere in the car with her. On and on, until the day was finally brought to an end.

She packed up her briefcase, said goodbye to her assistant and left the building.

The sun was still bright in the sky when she exited. Imogen collected her car from the nearby parking garage, turned into heavy traffic, drove over the Sydney Harbor Bridge and, rushed toward Manly.

She turned into the underground car park of the apartment building where she lived with Aaron and pulled into her space. She stepped from the car, closed the door and tapped the button on the remote control attached to her keys. The cheeping noise echoed in the deserted carpark. She ran for the lift, anxious to be in Sir's arms.

She pushed the button to call down the exclusive penthouse elevator. The bell dinged as the car settled in front of her and the doors whooshed open. She stepped inside and pushed the button for the top floor. Just a few minutes more.

The bell dinged again as the elevator settled onto her floor and the doors opened. She crossed the hall quickly, turned her key in the lock and stepped into the darkened apartment.

***

A large hand whipped across her mouth while another snaked under her skirt to rest between her ass and her pussy. The familiar scent of Aramis wafted up her nose and Imogen relaxed.

Aaron withdrew both of his hands and stalked off.

Underwear. Fuck. Aaron hated underwear. She always removed it in the car park, but she had been distracted by the court case and forgotten.

Imogen padded to their bedroom to remove her clothes. She was worried. Last time she had disobeyed Aaron he hadn't touched or spoken to her for three days. It had been hell on earth until he had forgiven her. At the beginning of such an important trial, she couldn't afford to be upset.

She stripped off her gray linen suit and hung it neatly in the wardrobe. Aaron was very particular about clothes being put away neatly at the end of the day. She stripped off her white cotton blouse, removed her gray leather shoes and rolled off her stockings.

She was standing in her favorite black lacy panties and plunge bra when Aaron strode in. She smiled at his glorious nakedness, his cock rigid against his flat belly. When she caught sight of the scissors in his hand, her heart sank.

The movement was swift as he snipped the side of her panties, the straps and front of her bra. The ruined garments floated to the floor.

"Sir...."

He raised his hand to silence her. "You are going to be punished for entering this home with underwear on. Do you understand this is not acceptable?"

"Y...yes, Sir."

"Turn around."

Imogen swiveled around, her heart pounded in anticipation. If Aaron knew how much she loved to be punished, he might not have obliged. She faced the side of the huge king sized bed.

Aaron tied a blindfold tightly around her eyes, effectively blackening her world. He then spread her legs wide using his knee.

"Bend over."

She bent over and rested her upper torso on the bed, ass high in the air. She waited.

"Such nice globes. You have a beautiful ass and it is about to be turned pink."

Imogen quivered with want.

When the first crack of the wooden paddle connected with her right ass cheek, Imogen gritted her teeth. To make any sound would stop the much wanted punishment.

The second slap was harder and it took all her strength to remain silent. The third and fourth slaps became progressively harder and her tender ass stung. When the fifth, and hardest slap connected, she could no longer control herself and a soft whimper of pleasure escaped.

She heard Aaron throw the paddle to the floor. "Stand up."

Once she was standing he spun her around, lifted her up and placed her down on the bed. He spread her legs and strapped them to the bottom of the bed frame. "Masturbate. Let me watch you pleasure yourself."

Imogen felt uncomfortable masturbating with her master watching but she knew better than to refuse. She spread the petals of her vagina and began stimulating her clitoris. She became instantly wet and within seconds, was drenched. Writhing and moaning, she began bringing herself toward a much-needed climax.

"You almost there?"

"Yes, Sir." Her voice shook with arousal.

Aaron captured her hands and fastened them above her head to the headboard.

Imogen wailed. "Please, Aaron. I was about to come." She heard him stomp from the room. She was left with the agony of almost being pleasured.

She continued to writhe and pinch her ass cheeks tightly together in an effort to satisfy herself. It was all to no avail.

***

Aaron stepped up to the refrigerator and helped himself to a beer. His cock was so hard he could have used it to pound nails. He had slapped Imogen so hard the vibration from the paddle had resonated up his arm but it wasn't until the fifth crack, she had broken.

Damn, he had wanted to fuck her senseless but she had to learn. He suspected his Sub enjoyed her punishment far more than she should. He took a long swallow of his beer and began running his free hand up and down his cock, he needed relief. His head lolled back in delight as the sensation heightened and cum poured from the tip. He slid down the wall and onto the floor as his knees gave way. Fuck, he felt good. He would be able to continue with Imogen without giving in to his manly desire.

Imogen lay still on the bed hoping Aaron would return soon and put her out of her misery. Her body was trembling with unspent desire.

When she felt something touch her belly, she lifted towards it. She was hoping whatever it was would travel further south.

"Sir?"

Aaron growled and again left the room. When would she learn? She knew not to speak unless given permission; she knew not to touch him without permission. He had gone over the list when she had first agreed to be his Sub, over two years ago, he had repeatedly reminded her when she made a mistake. "No more, from now on it would be punishment only. She has had long enough to learn." He muttered to himself.

He strode to his gym and began his usual one hour daily workout. He would leave her wondering.

Imogen cringed when she heard Aaron leave. "I am such a fool," she chastised. "Do not speak without permission. Unless, it's an emergency."

As she lay in her darkened world, she thought about being a Sub to Aaron's Dom. How did a thirty-year-old, brilliant lawyer end up being so Submissive in private? The fact was, she enjoyed being Dominated. Her work demanded she was Dominant in her everyday practice, it was freeing to Submit to her master when she was home.

Chapter Two

When Aaron returned to the bedroom after his workout and shower, Imogen slept peacefully. He knew she was exhausted after the first day of the trial, but he wasn't finished with his disobedient Sub yet.

He leaned over her slender body and captured a nipple into his mouth. She moaned as he laved it with his tongue and bit down gently on the tip. The other nipple then received the same treatment. They were both pebbled, the centers elongated when he sat on the edge of the bed and attached nipple clamps. Once in place, he tugged gently on the chain which connected them. This elicited writhing and moaning from his now wide awake Sub.

Imogen felt the pressure of the clamps and when Aaron tugged on the chain a burst of deSire shot straight to her core. She needed to be fucked. The constant arousal was maddening.

"What do you say?" Aaron asked softly.

"Fuck me please, Sir."

"What?"

Imogen groaned. "Forgive me please, Sir."

"Better."

"What won't you do again?"

"I won't wear underwear in the apartment."

"Very good."

"Now, what do you want?"

"Please, Sir. Fuck me."

"How?"

"I don't care." The minute the words were out, she regretted them. She had to learn to tell him exactly what she wanted. He had a devious mind and she never knew what he would come up with next.

Aaron padded from the room but returned within a few minutes.

Imogen felt the coldness as he pried the lips of her vagina open and thrust in an iced dildo. Her pussy contracted as Aaron slid the now melting toy in and out.

Her head thrashed from one side to the other as Aaron fucked Imogen's hot pussy with the ice dildo he had made earlier. His cock stiffened at the sight and cum began to drip from the tip. He withdrew the dildo and straddled her chest.

Imogen stifled a groan when Aaron removed the teasing dildo on the verge of her orgasm. How did he always know when she was about to shatter apart? She used all her restraint to remain silent.

"Open your mouth."

Imogen did as commanded and his rock-hard dick thrust down her throat. She could taste his juices as he lifted back, sliding his cock almost out of her eager mouth. He continued sliding out to the edge before plunging back in. Her tongue danced up the sides, teased his thickened veins and thrust into the slit of his cum-soaked tip. Aaron thrust faster and faster, his hands tangled in her hair causing pleasurable tingles. He exploded with a roar. His orgasm flowed down her throat as his satisfied dick lay in her mouth. She lapped hungrily at his juices, some running over her chin.

Imogen gave the best mouth fuck of any Aaron had ever had. She could take him deeper than he had ever been taken before and the fact she couldn't touch him made the experience even more arousing. He was in complete control.

He withdrew his dick from her mouth and rose from the bed. She heard him leave the room. *What now?* If she didn't come soon, she was sure she would explode.

She was startled when he began untying her feet. Surely, he wasn't going to leave her feeling like this? *I will lock the bathroom door and fuck myself.*

It was forbidden to bring herself to relief without his permission, but she didn't care, she was desperate enough to defy him.

He untied her hands from the headboard but held them together. "Stand."

Imogen scooted off the bed and stood, the soles of her feet caressed by the soft, thick carpet.

Aaron led her across the room and tied her hands to a ring which hung from the ceiling. Her feet barely touched the floor. He tore the nipple clamps from her tits and painful delight rocketed through her.

He lifted her legs to surround his slim waist and she locked her feet tight as he thrust his deSire-hardened cock into her. He thrust deeper and deeper, faster and faster until finally she burst over the edge. The orgasm tore through her, she shuddered and bucked as wave after wave of release caused her to shatter. Her orgasms were always much more powerful when she was denied for a while. As much as she hated the denial, the waiting was always well worth it.

Aaron lowered her feet to the floor. She felt his warm breath near her ear as he whispered in a menacing tone. "Don't ever think about locking yourself in the bathroom and finger fucking without my permission. Your pussy belongs to me and I will dictate when you come. Understood?"

How the fuck did he know what had been on my mind? "Yes, Sir."

His hand caressed the side of her cheek and she leaned into it. He kissed her lips gently, untied her hands and removed her blindfold before walking away. "Have a shower and leave the door open. Dinner's in an hour."

"Yes, Sir." Imogen tiptoed into the large bathroom which lay off the bedroom.

Half way through soothing her body under the hot water, Aaron joined her. Gathering Imogen into his arms, he rested her back against the wall and thoroughly fucked her again.

Imogen sighed. She felt wonderful.

Aaron grabbed a washcloth and squirted her favorite body wash into it. He roamed her body with the cloth, a soapy trail left behind as he moved on. He soaped her breasts, tweaked her nipples, before continuing downward.

"Spread your legs."

Imogen responded immediately and he gently kissed her lips.

He washed her pussy thoroughly before kneeling and attending to her legs. He stood, unhooked the showerhead from the wall and rinsed her off. He then gave her a washcloth and his favorite body wash so she could wash him.

Imogen prepared the cloth and kissed Aaron before moving the cloth over his body. A body she worshiped. His muscles rippled, ropes of muscles placed in a v-pattern led to his cock. And, what a magnificent cock it was; thick, long and it filled her completely. She knelt on the tiled floor and ran her tongue over him ending with a flick over the pearl of pre-cum at his tip. The action elicited a moan and he pulled at her hair.

"Imogen." His voice wavered.

"Sir?"

"You are insatiable. You will be the death of me."

"Yes, Sir. Sorry, Sir."

He heard the smile in her voice. Mischievous minx. "No, you're not. Finish washing me and remind me later, I owe you a spanking for touching me without permission."

"Yes, Sir."

Aaron sighed. "What am I going to do with you?"

Imogen raised her eyes and gave him an innocent look. "Fuck me, Sir?"

A belly laugh erupted from him. "Stand up."

Imogen stood and he took the cloth from her hands before his lips crashed down on hers. He held her tightly against him. His cock flinched with arousal. When they drew apart, they were both breathless.

Aaron turned off the taps and led Imogen from the shower. He wrapped her in a large fluffy towel and dried her off thoroughly. He kissed her, spun her around and slapped her pink ass hard.

Imogen squealed.

"Go and start dinner. I'll dry off and be there in a moment."

"Yes, Sir."

Imogen scooted away. Aaron watched her delicious ass wiggle and smiled. His feelings for his Sub ran deeper than any he'd ever had. He dried off, combed his hair and headed for the kitchen where they finished preparing dinner together.

***

Aaron heard the shower being turned on early the following morning and after pulling himself from the bed, he strode in to join Imogen.

He leaned against the glass panel as she washed. "You're up early."

Imogen jumped in surprise. "I have papers to get ready before I begin the cross-examination today. They should have been done last night but I was distracted."

Aaron laughed and stepped in under the water. He lifted her left leg and thrust his now hardened cock deep within her as he captured her lips.

Imogen found herself pushed up hard onto the wall as their movements became more and more frantic. They fell over the ledge of satisfaction together and when Aaron slid to the floor, he pulled Imogen with him. She straddled his lap, his still solid cock buried deep inside her. He began suckling her pebbled nipples and a full-blown arousal resulted. Once again, they found ecstasy together.

"Sir, I have to get to the Courthouse," she whispered. She wanted to stay and play but worried she would be late.

"I won't allow you to be late. I know how important this case is to your career. As your master, I would never allow that part of your life to be jeopardized. The clock is one hour fast to allow us to play before you have to leave. As you were up early, there is even more time which will allow you to go over your papers." Aaron rose and pulled her to her feet. He then began soaping her body. "Your body is exquisite and mine but, Imogen."

"Yes, Sir."

"You must tell me when you have work. As much as I want to fuck you all day and all night, I will not allow you to put important work aside. You have my permission, actually, I *insist* you tell me when you have papers or briefings to review."

"Thank you, Sir." Imogen stood on tiptoe and kissed her master.

Once washed he led her from the shower and dried her. "Go and lay on the bed." He kissed the tip of her nose.

Imogen didn't argue. She padded over and lay on the bed.

"Roll onto your stomach."

She rolled over and heard Aaron rummaging in a drawer. A chest of drawers nearby housed their toys. Aaron ensured they were all cleaned, sterilized and put back into place after each was used.

He lifted her ass with one hand and gently inserted a butt plug. Imogen squirmed.

She always found the feeling of fullness and the constant arousal plugs provoked, distracting.

Aaron pulled her from the bed and onto her feet. He grinned as she frowned with confusion. "My disobedient Sub. You will *not* wear underwear today and the plug will remain in all day."

Imogen cringed. She was in court for fuck's sake. How would she manage with being aroused all day? "But...."

Aaron placed his fingers over her lips before kissing her gently. "Get dressed and I will drive you to work. I'll pick you up when you break for lunch and we'll go to the hotel."

Aaron kept a room at the Boulevard Hotel across the road. There was no way she could remove the damn plug and slip on her underwear. He would walk her into court and return to pick her up. She would just have to cope. The idea of wearing a plug in court excited her.

The car ride into work was excruciatingly long. The plug stimulated her core every time Aaron hit a bump in the road. She was sure he deliberately hit as many bumps as possible. By the time they arrived at the parking lot near the courthouse, Imogen was drenched, as she knew she would be. She cleaned the juices away with a hand towel she had brought with her.

***

Aaron held her hand as he walked her around to the front of the courthouse. "My sweet, have a good day. I hope everything goes well." He leaned over and kissed her while sliding his hand under her skirt and tweaking the plug. Imogen thought she would melt into a puddle of desire. She scowled as he strolled away laughing.

Imogen mounted the court steps with trepidation. It was going to be a very long day.

Maybe, Aaron would allow her to remove the butt plug when they made love in the lunch break. *Pigs might fly!*

"Miss Walters," Madison greeted with a smirk on his face.

Does he know? Of course, he doesn't, don't be so stupid. "Good morning, Mr. James."

"I have a couple more questions for my client and then you may cross," he informed her.

Imogen nodded. They had agreed that he would begin questioning with his client and then she would present the prosecutions' case. After that, Defence would present their case in full.

They watched as the jury filed in. They were asked to rise for the judge. She was thankful, she hadn't had to sit down on the hard chair, *yet.* The judge took his seat and it could no longer be avoided. Imogen sat and the sensation from the plug almost caused her to squeal.

Keep still and it won't turn you on. Easier said than done. She had no idea what had been said and the judge was forced to call her name loudly when her turn to ask questions came. She stood gingerly knowing every slight movement would cause a burst of arousal.

She would normally have walked back and forth when questioning a witness but she stood like a robot, not daring to move. She needed to concentrate and focus or this prick was going to walk free.

"Mr. Wright. When was the last time you saw the victim – Miss Linton?"

Timothy Wright raked his eyes over her body and licked his lips, she cringed with disgust.

She had gone from not liking the bastard to detesting him. It was as though he knew she was naked under her suit.

"Mr. Wright, please answer my question."

"Ummm, about a week before she died."

"Thank you, please step down." Timothy did as she asked giving her a smirk and making a show of flicking his tongue over his lips as he returned to his seat.

Imogen tried not to shudder. Revolting pig.

"Please call Kim Pitt to the stand."

Kim was sworn in and took her seat. Imogen had her well prepared.

"Miss Pitt, when did you last see the accused and the deceased together?"

"I saw them when he picked her up from work on the night of January 5."

"Are you sure it was January 5, the night she died?"

"Yes. I got a phone call from her mother at about 11pm asking if I had seen her. I told Mrs. Linton I had seen her being picked up by Timothy. The next morning, we found out she was dead." She dabbed at her eyes with a tissue.

"You saw Miss Linton go willingly with Mr. Wright?"

"Yes, they appeared to be discussing something, but he wasn't pulling her along or anything."

"You have been Miss Linton's friend since high school, is that correct?"

"Yes, Peta, Janet and me were close friends."

"Did Miss Linton tell you anything about her relationship with Mr. Wright?"

"Only that she was breaking it off because he was too demanding and controlling. He used to make her do things she didn't want to."

"Like what?"

"Janet was a virgin. He wanted her to do kinky sex things and she wouldn't let him, so he called her names. Once or twice he slapped her, it left her with bruises. I think she was scared of him."

"You are sure she hadn't changed her mind?"

"Absolutely. She would never have changed her mind. She wanted to save herself for whoever she married."

"Alright. Thank you, Miss Pitt. Your witness Mr. James."

Dalton rose slightly, "no questions."

"You may step down Miss Pitt," the judge instructed.

Aaron sat in the gallery watching. He was in awe of Imogen. She was brilliant and *his*. His cock jumped to attention at the thought he would be screwing her in just a few minutes.

"Miss Walters, Mr James. We will take a two-hour recess for lunch before commencing with the next witness." The judge banged his gavel as he stood and left the courtroom.

The jury filed from the room. Imogen shuffled papers into her briefcase. When she turned, Timothy Wright's eyes were locked on her. He mouthed, *I will come for you, fucking bitch.* She noticed the mad twinkling of his eyes before she fled from the room.

Aaron stood outside on the steps and she flew into his arms. "Take me to the hotel now, please, Sir."

Imogen was trembling which made Aaron both angry and fearful. She never called him Sir outside of their apartment. Something had happened, something was terribly wrong. He led her across the road, into the hotel and up to their room.

Chapter Three

Aaron guided Imogen into the bedroom and spun her into his arms. "Tell me, what happened?" She trembled against him.

"The defendant was staring at me like I was a piece of meat he wanted to devour. He really scares me, Aaron. He said he will come for me." Tears flowed over her cheeks.

"Can you talk to his lawyer, the Judge?"

"I don't think so. They probably would say, I imagined it. I know his lawyer would argue I was worried I was losing the case, so I made it up."

"I'll be in court with you every day until it's done. I won't have you upset or threatened." He held her close and kissed her tenderly before slowly undressing her.

Once she was naked, Aaron stripped off his clothes and pulled her down onto the bed with him. He caressed her nipples, placed light kisses all over her face and crooned to her. "I will not let him hurt you. I protect what is mine, you know that." He captured her lips and their tongues began a sensuous dance.

Within minutes her fear was forgotten. She trusted Aaron to protect her. Imogen's heated body was filled with deSire. She loved the hotel, this was where they were lovers. Dom and Sub left at the apartment.

She stroked her soft hand over his semi hard cock and it jumped to attention. Aaron needed to make more time to come here. He was worth millions now thanks to his Computer Software business. With a Manager in place he could do whatever, whenever he liked. He would love Imogen to give up the law so she could be only his but, he would never demand it. Maybe he would discuss it with her after this trial.

Aaron reached behind Imogen and twisted the butt plug. She bucked and almost came on the spot. Sitting up she straddled his dick and began gyrating her hips. He moaned with delight. As her actions became faster and they both began hitting the heights, he captured both her mouth and her screams of delight.

Their chests rose and fell rapidly as they lay side by side. For over an hour they had made love, both were exhausted.

"Aaron?"

"Hmmm?"

"May I take the plug out for this afternoon's session?"

Aaron sat up. "Are you saying you want to be released from your punishment early? I know how much you hate it. I think having the plug in while being in public is the only damn punishment that works on you. I know it brings you to the edge of orgasm constantly but you disobeyed me."

"Yes, Sir. I am sorry, Sir." Imogen knew better than to argue or even plead. She would have to find a way to deal with it. One thing was for certain, she would try hard not to disobey again while the trial was in session.

It was the first time Aaron had dealt out this punishment while she was in court and, he was right, she hated it.

***

After showering and dressing, Aaron walked Imogen back to court. She couldn't wait for the day to be over and the stimulating plug to be removed. Their safe word – 'Yellow Rose' – could have been used and Aaron would have allowed removal of the damn thing, but Imogen hated to admit defeat so, it stayed. Damn her stubbornness.

She averted her eyes as she entered the courtroom, but she was aware of Timothy Wright watching her every step. The hairs on the back of her neck stood on end. The sooner this trial was over, the better.

She removed papers from her briefcase and, while she waited for the judge and the jury to return, Imogen read over what she had planned for the afternoon session. Her assistant placed a glass of cold water on the desk before her and sat in the chair beside her.

As before, everyone in the court was instructed to stand. The jury was led in and the judge strode to his seat.

Once all were seated and the room became quiet, Imogen moved forward and called her next witness. "Miss Peta Caine, please step forward."

Peta Caine, a small, slender girl appeared terrified as she approached and took her vow to be truthful. Once she was seated, Imogen approached.

"It's okay, Miss Caine. Just relax. I would like you to tell the court when you last saw your friend, the deceased, Janet Linton."

"I saw her at a party at Kim's place on the Friday night before she died."

"Did you get the news she was dead the following Tuesday morning?"

"Yes, Kim phoned me after she heard from Janet's mother."

"Who was Janet with at the party?"

"She came with Tim but talked to everyone."

"Mr. Wright said he hadn't seen her for at least a week, one of you must be mistaken?"

"He's lying." Peta scowled at Timothy Wright. He smirked, turned to his lawyer and whispered something. The lawyer nodded.

"Okay, thank you, Miss Caine. Your witness Mr. James.

"I have no questions," Mr. James said.

"Mr. Sean Murray, please step forward," Imogen commanded.

Sean Murray, a Sydney business owner, placed his hand on the proffered Bible and swore to tell the truth before being asked to sit.

Imogen moved toward him. She began pacing but stopped abruptly when the butt plug reminded her of its presence. "Mr. Murray, you were present at the Jailhouse Bar on the night of January 5 this year. Is that correct?"

"Yes ma'am, I was."

"Do you see anyone in this room that was also there on January 5 this year?"

"Yes, ma'am. Pete Young, my friend and the accused." Sean pointed out both men.

"Did you have occasion to talk with Mr. Wright?"

"Yes. He joined us at our table with his drink just after 10pm. The bar was pretty full and we had two spare seats."

"Did you notice anything unusual?"

"He had, what looked like blood, smeared on the shoulder of his shirt."

"Do you know where it came from?"

"No, I thought maybe it was wine spilled on him. I asked what it was and he said he'd cut himself shaving. I couldn't see any shaving cuts, but it was fairly dark in the club. I thought it was strange that he hadn't changed his shirt before coming to the club. "

"Anything else you can remember noticing?"

"He kept looking around. Like he was watching for someone."

"How long were you there?"

"We left about an hour later. He was still at the table."

"Your witness, Mr. James."

"No questions."

Yeah, your case is unraveling, jerk. "You may step down, Mr. Murray." Imogen rewarded the young man with a smile.

Aaron watched from the gallery. He had seated himself in a dark corner of the back row to ensure he wouldn't distract Imogen but where he was able to keep his eye on her.

"One more witness for today, Miss Walters." Judge O'Malley directed.

"Yes, Sir. I would like to call Mr. Peter Young to the stand."

With the swearing in completed, Peter turned his radiant smile towards Imogen.

Aaron seethed.

"Mr. Young, can you remember where you were on January 5 this year?"

"I was at the Jailhouse Bar. Me and Sean were cruising the place for chicks."

Imogen chose to ignore his comment about 'chicks'. "Do you remember seeing the accused there that night?"

"What night?"

Great, a dumb one that thinks with his dick. "January 5 this year."

"Oh yeah. That's right. Me and Sean seen him. He was kinda nervous and Sean said he had blood on his shirt."

Madison James bounced up from behind his desk. "Objection, hearsay."

Yep, saw that coming. Imogen sighed. "Mr. Young please stick to what *you* saw."

"Sorry."

"That's alright, no further questions. Mr. James?"

Madison stood and moved close to the young man. "Mr. Young, how many drinks had you consumed on the night of January 5 this year?"

"I don't know. I was drinkin' rum and I was pretty drunk. Sean had to get me home before I puked."

The gallery laughed.

Imogen groaned.

"So, you wouldn't know if my client was in the bar or not? You wouldn't know if he had blood on his shoulder or a pink elephant?"

Imogen stood. "Objection. Derogatory."

Madison James snorted with disgust. "No further questions."

Imogen stood again. You may step down Mr. Young."

"Okay. Thanks, Miss Walters, thanks Judge." The young man rejoined his friend.

"I call an end to proceedings for the day. Court will resume at 10am tomorrow." The judge stood and was whisked from the courtroom.

Aaron slipped out to meet Imogen at the front of the building. Imogen packed up her briefcase, wished all a goodnight and took her leave.

She stepped into the balmy warmth of the evening. Aaron stood waiting at the bottom of the steps and she rushed to him.

***

Aaron and Imogen strolled to the car park hand in hand.

"How did your interviews go today?" Imogen was aware that Aaron was selecting a new Assistant Manager and he had scheduled several interviews in his city office during the afternoon.

"I got through them fairly quick and was able to come back and watch your case. I don't want you left alone."

"I didn't see you and I'm hardly alone in a packed courthouse."

"I sat in the back corner so I wouldn't distract or unnerve you. You never know when the judge might end the day early and I promised to keep you safe. I saw you smile at those young male witnesses."

Imogen tensed. She was well aware of Aaron's jealous streak. "It was just a smile. You know I'm yours."

"I still didn't like it."

"I can't be a sourpuss with everyone just because you don't like me smiling at them."

"I guess, but I still didn't like it."

Imogen patted his arm as they reached the car. "The only smiles that mean something are those I give you."

He placed a kiss on her lips and opened the door for her. She slipped onto the cool leather seat.

Aaron carved through the traffic like a seasoned racing car driver and in no time at all he pulled into the parking spot next to her Mercedes.

He stepped around and opened her door, offered her his hand and pulled her into his arms. As he placed a kiss on her lips, he lifted her skirt and twisted the plug.

Imogen gasped. Her nipples stood to attention and her entire body trembled with deSire. "Inside please," she panted.

Once inside the apartment, Aaron kicked the door shut and headed to the kitchen. Imogen made her way to the bedroom.

By the time he approached the bedroom, she was naked and presented on her knees at the side of the doorway.

"Stand." It was more an order than a request. Sir had returned.

"On the bed, face up."

Imogen lay on the bed watching Aaron strip. He was magnificent. His skin had an all over golden glow, muscles bunched up and down his arms, across his chest and in his thighs with every movement he made.

"Are you watching me?"

Imogen lowered her eyes but it was too late, he had seen her staring in awe.

He crawled onto the bed and lifted her onto her knees before slipping in behind her.

Aaron cuffed her wrists together before he began kneading her breasts roughly. She pushed into his hands.

"How many orgasms did you have today?"

Imogen tried to remember. "S...six, Sir."

Quick as a flash she was rolled onto her belly, pulled onto her knees and a hard slap stung her ass. "How many *satisfying* orgasms did you have?"

Shit, he means the ones he gave me. "Four, Sir. Two before work and two at lunch time."

"How many will you have tonight?"

"As many as Sir would like to give me."

"He withdrew the butt plug and Imogen felt a sense of release."

Aaron positioned one of his legs over her back. She could feel the hardness of his cock as it pressed into her hip. He slid two fingers in and out of her anus and at the same time he teased her clit. Her orgasm was building and Imogen began bucking.

Aaron stopped. He pushed himself from the bed and moved away.

Imogen bit her lip to keep from groaning. She wanted to reach down and finish the job for herself.

She almost laughed with relief when Aaron returned to the bed. He pushed a vibrating dildo inside her pussy before gently filling her ass with his cock.

Their bucking became frenzied as they both reached for the heavens. Aaron wrapped her hair in his fists, pulled her head back and roared as they both came together.

"Mine," he growled before collapsing beside her.

Imogen lay exhausted but finally satisfied after being teased to distraction all afternoon.

Chapter Four

Imogen moved around the kitchen preparing a salad while Aaron stirred the soup. Both remained naked and now and then he would grab her and tease her pussy causing juices to drip to her thighs. A washcloth strategically placed on the bench came in handy.

He whispered in her ear, "I have more planned for you. Do you have anything to go over tonight?"

"Not tonight. I've done all I can now." A shiver of anticipation raced down her spine.

As they sat at the polished oak dining table, sipping red wine and eating their dinner, they discussed the events of the day.

"Did you hire someone to be the Assistant to Adam?" Imogen asked.

"Hmmm, I have someone in mind," Aaron answered as he refilled their glasses.

"What's he like?"

Aaron glared at her from beneath hooded eyelids. *Shit.* "I meant, what are *they* like?"

"Too late. Do you think it might be someone you can fuck?"

"Don't talk such rubbish. I made an assumption." Imogen's temper surfaced.

Aaron decided to have fun. "I actually have a woman in mind. Slim, mid 20s, longest legs I've ever seen."

It was Imogen's turn to glare. She slammed down her fork and pushed her plate away as she stood.

"Get in the bedroom."

"No. You'll stop fucking before I climax. It leaves me frustrated and I'm sick of it, *SIR.*"

Her sassy attitude rubbed Aaron the wrong way. He sprang from his chair and it crashed to the floor with a loud bang.

Imogen raced for the bedroom. *Shit, now I've done it.* Excitement washed over her. She loved pushing her boundaries and seeing how Aaron would react.

Aaron stormed into the room, wrenched open a drawer and withdrew a paddle.

"I'm sorry, Sir," Imogen muttered from the other side of the bed. But, she was far from it.

"Get on the fucking bed, now!"

Imogen leaped onto the bed.

Aaron turned her onto her belly, strapped her hands to the headboard and feet to the base. He grabbed a handful of hair and pulled her head back toward him. "I have told you, I won't tolerate your sassiness. His words were growled, but the slight curl to his lips betrayed how he felt. He enjoyed her defiance."

"Yes, Sir."

"What am I?"

"My master."

"What are you?"

"Your Sub."

"Who makes the decisions?"

"You do, Sir."

"Do you want to leave?"

Aaron had never asked that question before. Imogen panicked. Was he going to replace her? *Please don't let me have pushed him too far.*

"Aaron, please. I don't want to leave."

Imogen felt the sting of the paddle as it hit her right cheek.

"Is that the right answer?"

"No, Sir. No, I don't want to leave."

"Is it my decision who I hire?"

"Yes, Sir. I was jealous."

The paddle came down hard on her left cheek and she yelped. That earned her two further slaps.

"Did I ask if you were jealous?"

"No, Sir."

"If I think a woman is the right one for the job, I will hire her. Is that clear?"

"Yes, Sir."

Four further slaps of the paddle left Imogen's backside throbbing deliciously.

Aaron untied her, flipped her onto her back and secured her once more.

"Open, your mouth."

Imogen's mouth fucked his cock until he was satisfied. She hoped he would no longer be angry.

He untied her straps.

"Go and have a shower."

Imogen crawled off the bed and padded off to the bathroom.

Aaron followed the sway of her hips, her backside glowed pink. He had no intention of hiring the female, she wasn't right for the job. But, she didn't need to know that just yet. How dare she question his loyalty?

***

Imogen flinched as the hot water hit her stinging ass. Why was it, the rougher the treatment, the more turned on she became? She knew Aaron wouldn't stay angry for long.

She loved to provoke him, but he had genuinely scared her when he had asked if she wanted to leave.

Aaron slipped into the shower and wrapped her in his arms. He placed kisses over her face and down onto her shoulder. "Turn around and touch your toes."

Imogen complied, and within seconds his hard dick penetrated. It was all she could do to keep her knees straight and not collapse in a heap on the floor. This man certainly knew how to make her feel good.

His pumping settled into a rhythm and Imogen was just on the verge of a climax when he withdrew.

"Suck me until I come," he commanded.

Imogen knelt and took him into her mouth, her hands firmly locked at her back. He hadn't given her permission to touch him. She felt the first trickles of cum before he exploded, and it flowed down her throat. When she glanced up he smirked. He knew how frustrated she was feeling.

When you are finished I want you outside on the deck.

"Yes, Sir."

"Naked, Imogen."

"But …" She stopped when he glared at her.

Imogen finished her shower and made her way onto the deck. Aaron was dressed and waiting.

"Lie on the deck chair."

A towel had been placed on the chair and Imogen positioned herself on it.

He pulled her legs to each side and tied them apart. He then tied her hands above her head and secured them to the base of the chair. She was unable to move. The warm evening air caressed her body and caused her nipples to peak before Aaron closed the shutters for privacy.

Aaron wrapped a blindfold around her eyes and placed a gag in her mouth before slipping inside. What was he doing?

A few seconds after he returned, Imogen felt something prodding at her pussy. It was a large dildo. He switched it on to slow vibrate and Imogen instantly became excited.

She heard a deck chair squeak as Aaron sat down. She knew he was watching as the dildo brought his Sub to a mind-blowing climax. Juices flooded from her and she writhed and bucked as much as she could with the restrictions he had placed on her.

Imogen felt like she was flying. It was one of the best orgasms she had experienced without Aaron. She was exhausted but the dildo continued to vibrate and tease. Another orgasm built in no time and she felt herself explode. Still the dildo vibrated relentlessly. She was beginning to feel sorry she had complained. No amount of bucking, squirming or writhing would slow the damn thing down and she was forced to shoot for the stars again and again.

Aaron watched her carefully. It had been thirty minutes and she was obviously becoming distressed with the constant stimulation. He withdrew the gag. "Have you had enough?" He certainly had, his dick felt like it had a permanent hard-on and it was beginning to ache.

"Yes, Sir. Please stop," she begged. Tears trickled from her eyes.

Aaron switched off the vibrator and withdrew it. After untying her, he sent her straight to bed. He then proceeded to fuck her until he found his own relief. It would be a long time before she complained about not having an orgasm again.

Chapter Five

6 January 2012

18 months earlier

Senior Detective John Morgan and Detective Ryan Kahn knelt down and inspected the body of a young girl. She had been found dead in Nolan Reserve off Pittwater Road by a couple out walking their dog. The area had been cordoned off by the police to protect any evidence.

John ran his fingers through his hair as he stood up. Ryan joined him and they strode toward the Coroner.

"Cause of death, Doc?" John asked Dr. Marie Antopolous.

"Blunt force trauma to the side of the head. Epidural Haematoma, I would guess until I examine her further."

"Any evidence nearby?" Ryan directed his question to the two young officers who had been first to arrive at the scene.

"Not that we could see, Sir." The shorter of the two answered.

"What do you think it was caused by, Doc?"

"A wooden board, piece of pipe, cricket bat. Hard to say until we do an autopsy, but it would be one of those." She held up a sliver of wood. "This was protruding from the wound.

"Thanks." John and Ryan moved back to the victim.

John lifted her hands and inspected her fingernails. It would be too much to expect to find skin but he had to check. He scanned the ground from where the body was lying on the roadside and frowned.

Ryan checked the rest of the victim's once beautiful body. No scrapes, bruises or bumps. "Looks like just the one blow to the head, John."

"It's a damn shame." John signaled for the ambulance officers who had been patiently waiting nearby. "Take her away and tell the morgue to let me know as soon as they have an ID."

After the body was removed, John, Ryan and several officers combed the reserve searching for clues. There was nothing.

After more than four hours, John called everyone together. "Anything?"

They all shook their heads.

"Don't you think it's strange that the grass is only flattened by one set of footprints? There was a heavy dew last night and the grass would have been wet. It flattened easily. It tells me she was perhaps murdered somewhere else and carried here."

"Let's get back to the station, hopefully we'll have an ID on her soon."

***

"John, we got an ID on that victim." The desk Sergeant called him over. "It's twenty-three-year-old Janet Linton. Parents have been contacted and came down and identified the body about ten minutes ago. This is the address. They said to drop by anytime, they aren't going anywhere and they want their daughter's killer found."

John took the paper with the address scrawled across it. "Thanks, Bill. Ryan, come with me."

The two men left, climbed into a police car and drove toward Manly where the young victim's parents lived. When they arrived at the front door to their home, John and Ryan introduced themselves and were invited in.

"Take a seat, officers." A white-faced, strained looking Tony Linton indicated the lounge and both men sat.

"We are very sorry for your loss, Mr. Linton. We know you don't feel much like answering questions, so we will make it brief." John hated this part of the job. The man he was facing appeared extremely distressed which was understandable.

"I just want the bastard who did this, caught and locked up. I bet Timothy Wright has something to do with this. Thinks because he's the Mayors' son he can get away with anything, including murder. Janet told him time and time again she wouldn't have sex with him. He slapped her around a couple of times and she told her mother and me she was going to get rid of him."

"Whoa, that's a pretty big accusation," John warned.

"No-one else would have harmed our little girl. It's him you should question."

"We will but we need to ask you a couple of questions first. Where did your daughter go last night?" Ryan asked.

"Her friend, Kim Pitt, who she works with, said Tim picked Janet up from work. She saw them walking to the car park near the girl's office."

John sat back and allowed Ryan to do the questioning. "Did she say if they were fighting, was he dragging her?"

"Not according to Kim. I asked if Janet had been taken by force and she assured me she hadn't."

"When did you find out she had gone with Mr. Wright?"

"My wife, Kellyanne, phoned Kim at about 11pm. She was worried when Janet hadn't come home. Sometimes she would stay out all night but she was a good girl and we trusted her."

"If she sometimes stayed out, why were you worried?"

"Her mother was worried because Janet didn't tell us. She always told us if she wouldn't be home or if something unexpected came up, she phoned us."

"Okay. Thanks, Mr. Linton. That will be all for now. Where is your wife?"

"Doc gave her a sedative and she went to bed. She was on the verge of collapse. Janet was our only child." Tears filled the man's eyes.

"We understand." The Detectives stood and shook hands with Tony. He showed them out and they radioed in for Timothy Wright's address.

Chapter Six

Imogen awoke just on daybreak and rolled toward Aaron. He pulled her on top of his body and kissed her gently.

"Good morning, my girl."

"Good morning, Master."

He ran his hands down her body as she stretched out on top of him.

She felt his morning wood press into her belly and shivered in anticipation. Aaron rolled her over and hovered above her. He made slow, gentle, love to her and by the time they left the apartment, she was glowing with happiness.

They chatted about what was planned for the day as Aaron negotiated the traffic into the city. "Have you had any more comments from that prick?"

"No, but he scares me. I don't know what it is about him, but I think he's dangerous."

Aaron patted her bare thigh. "He can't hurt you. They will probably throw him in jail for a very long time."

She turned her face and for a second they locked eyes. The love he felt for her shone from his sparkling blue eyes and her heart skipped a beat. He hadn't told her he loved her but he showed her in so many ways. Imogen had decided, she wouldn't tell Aaron how deeply in love with him she was until he voiced the words.

"I will be in the gallery on and off, but I have to go into the office and tie up a few loose ends. I will be at the courthouse well before the lunch break and we will spend time at the hotel."

"Thank you, Aaron."

"How about we go out for dinner after I pick you up tonight."

"I would love to." She leaned over and kissed his cheek.

They pulled into the dark of the underground car park and he drew her into his arms for a long, sensuous kiss. "Better get your bra and panties on while no-one is around. I can't believe you left them off."

"I wanted to please, Sir." She bared her top half, clipped on her bra and replaced her blouse. She then pulled on a lacy thong and giggled as Aaron licked his lips.

He walked her up to the courthouse door and gathered her into his arms for a kiss. "Aaron, people."

"Mine," he stated before striding away.

***

The courtroom was packed, it was the day the police would give evidence and a lot of people were anxious to hear the details of how Timothy Wright had come to be charged.

"Order, order." The judge banged his gavel to quieten everyone down. "Miss Walters, call your next witness."

"I call Detective John Morgan to the stand."

John lumbered to where the clerk stood with the Bible and swore to tell the truth before taking his seat.

"Detective Morgan, you were one of the first Officers at the scene where the deceased was found?"

"Yes, I was called in by the beat police. Detective Ryan Kahn and I arrived at the scene about twenty minutes after the initial call came in from a couple walking their dog."

"What did you find?"

"We studied the victim and spoke with the Coroner. She, Doctor Marie Antopolous, said the victim had blunt force trauma to the temple. I checked under her nails for skin, thought she might have scratched her attacker, but her nails and fingers were clean."

"Please tell the court what else you found."

John turned toward the jury. "There had been a heavy dew the night before. The grass was flattened between the road and the bushes where the victim was found but only by one person. This led me to believe the victim was murdered elsewhere and dumped at the reserve later."

"What prompted you to speak with the accused?" Imogen turned to face Timothy and noticed the Mayor glaring at her from the gallery above him. The look in his eyes was pure lust. A chill raced down her spine. *Like father, like fucking son.*

"We spoke to the victim's father. He informed us, Janet had been having problems with the accused because she had refused his sexual advances. Mr. Linton said she was about to break off their relationship."

"It makes sense you would talk to him but what made you suspicious, why was he charged?"

"Mr. Linton told us his daughter had been collected from work by the accused and no-one had seen or heard from her after that. Mr. Wright stated he hadn't seen her for over a week, but when we questioned her friends and witnesses who came forward, they all said she was seen with him just after 5.30pm on the night she was murdered. He had picked her up from her place of work."

"Thank you. Mr. James, your witness." Imogen sat at her desk.

"Detective, you say my client was with the victim on the night of the murder, but that doesn't prove he killed her. What evidence do you have? You already told the court there was no sign of a struggle, no skin under her nails, no scratches on my client."

"We spoke to some people at the club where Mr. Wright said he was after 10pm. They verified the time and said he looked disheveled. They also said there was blood on his shirt, on his shoulder."

"Did you match the blood off the shirt with the victim's blood?"

"No, Sir. The accused had already washed the shirt and the lab couldn't get enough blood residue to test."

"So Detective, in other words, you have no evidence except the word of a few inebriated patrons at a bar?"

"We know he was with her and no-one saw her after that. We were also told he was abusive toward her."

"That, detective, does not equate to murder. No further questions."

Madison James had caused a setback for Imogen, but as she packed up to leave for the lunch break, she still felt confident.

***

"How did it go?" Aaron was waiting out front. He gathered her hand into his and led her across the busy road to the hotel.

"I thought the Detective's evidence was pretty convincing, but Madison James threw a lot of doubt over it."

"Yes, I was in the gallery. He did a good job of making the jury question Wright's guilt."

Aaron slipped a key card into the door and drew Imogen inside the luxurious hotel room.

A table had been set with all sorts of delicacies - caviar, oysters, other fresh seafood and a vase of fresh flowers took pride of place in the center.

Imogen twisted, stood on her toes and drew Aaron's head down. She captured his lips in a lingering kiss. She loved romantic Aaron. "Thank you."

"Do you want to eat first or fuck?" One side of his mouth tilted upward in a sexy smile she couldn't resist.

"Lead me to your boudoir please, Sir," she answered cheekily.

He scooped her into his arms and strode to the bedroom. After laying her on the huge, king sized bed, he began slowly undressing her. He planted kisses over her body as each section was bared.

Imogen pulled at the buttons of his shirt, but he pushed her away.

"Slowly, we have almost three hours and I want to pleasure you first."

He drew off her panties and pushed two thick fingers deep inside her always receptive pussy. She was drenched and ready. He massaged her clit as he sucked on her nipples. Imogen began writhing, her hands entwined in his hair.

"Please, Aaron. Fuck me."

He sat back on his haunches and lifted her feet up onto his shoulders. As he buried his head between her legs she locked her ankles at his neck, she was not letting him loose.

He began to devour her with his tongue. While the fingers of one hand assisted his tongue, the other hand tormented her body relentlessly.

She shuddered as his motions increased in pace and shattered into a million pieces.

Aaron slithered up her body and captured her mouth. He then stood and undressed. His thickened cock rested against his belly and Imogen could see the sheen of cum at the tip.

She held her arms out and he lowered himself to her. His cock slid into her well-prepared cunt and together they made love for more than an hour. The food was forgotten.

***

Imogen smiled as she walked into the empty courtroom after lunch. She was well and truly sated. When a hand dropped onto her arm, she spun around in shock. The Mayor glared at her.

"Please remove your hand from my arm," Imogen spoke bravely. She was trembling inside and wished she hadn't come back fifteen minutes early.

The Mayor ignored her and dragged her toward a private room at the rear.

"Where are you taking me? I will scream."

"Go ahead. I have spoken with court officials and postponed the rest of the days' trial until tomorrow. You are the only one allowed in." He laughed at the fear in her eyes.

"Let me go, you bastard." Imogen lowered her head and bit his hand. He immediately released her and she began running.

He reached out and grabbed a handful of hair which not only brought her to a stop but also to her knees. He dragged her across the floor and into the empty room.

Imogen kicked and screamed but to no avail. The Mayor held tight.

"Settle down you bitch. I want to talk to you."

"I have nothing to say to you."

The crack across her cheek was unexpected and her head snapped back. Stars danced before her eyes as he threw her onto a chair and bound her hands and feet.

He dabbed at the bite on his arm, clearing away the blood she had drawn. "Now, you are going to listen to me."

She glared up at him in defiance.

"You are going to drop the charges against my son. You can tell the Judge that a mistake was made and you no longer think he killed Janet."

"No fuckin' way. You can go to hell and I will make sure, not only your asshole son goes to jail, but you as well."

The Mayor walked to the door. When he opened it two vicious, giant-like *thugs* entered the room. Imogen shook with terror.

"These are my friends and if you don't do as I ask, they are going to pay you a nice little visit. By the time they finish *visiting,* your cunt will be so big it will be like screwing an open window for your boyfriend."

Imogen spat and caught the arrogant bastard in the face.

He stood and slapped her across the cheek. As he wiped the spit from his face, he nodded to his goons.

The larger of the two stood in front of her and dropped his pants. His cock was hard and was the largest she had ever seen. Aaron was big, but this man was abnormally huge. When he smiled, she noticed his rotten teeth and almost gagged.

He lowered his hand, pushed her skirt up to her hips and tore off her panties. *God no, they are going to rape me!*

He shoved his fingers inside her and she fought like a tiger. His long, jagged nails tore at her delicate skin and tears filled her eyes.

"Alright, I will do what you say."

The Mayor nodded, the man stepped back and zipped up his pants. The two men left the room.

"Very good." The Mayor picked up her panties and tucked them into his pocket. "If you say one word about this, we will find you. Before we do, though, I will go to the media and show them your panties. I will tell them you came onto me and fucked my brains out."

He untied Imogen and she fled from the room. She needed Aaron *now*.

Chapter Seven

Aaron was in his office, two blocks from the courthouse when his mobile phone rang. The caller ID showed Imogen's name and he frowned. She was in the middle of a trial, why was she calling?

"Imogen?"

"Aaron, I'm at the hotel. Please come as quick as you can."

She was crying hard and sobbing. Imogen *never* cried. She was the strongest person Aaron had ever known. He raced for the elevator. "I'm coming, baby." He ended the call, caught the elevator to the street and ran.

Aaron burst into the hotel room and Imogen flew into his arms. She clung to him as if her life depended on it.

"What happened? Why aren't you in court?" Aaron led her to the couch and they sat down. He prised her away from his chest and stared into her face. Angry, purple bruises covered her cheek and a small gash oozed blood. Her eyes were dull, lifeless and she was as pale as the dead. "What the fuck?" Aaron's knuckles gently grazed her cheek. "Who did this?" He was beyond angry. He wanted to kill the bastard who had hurt his love.

Imogen buried her head back in his chest, her body shook as she sobbed.

He ran his hand over her hair and her back, placed kisses on the top of her head and held her. She would talk when she was ready. *Whoever did this is dead.*

After what seemed like hours, but was actually around twenty minutes, Imogen settled. When she lifted her head and gazed into his eyes, his heart shattered. The hurt in her eyes was unbearable. He captured her mouth in the gentlest of kisses. He loved this woman. When had that happened? He had been with other Subs over the years, he was thirty-five years old and Imogen wasn't his first. She was the first he had fallen deeply in love with, though.

"The Mayor canceled court until tomorrow. He dragged me into a back room and th..threatened me. He wants me to drop the case."

Aaron dabbed at the tears on her face and pressed another gentle kiss to her lips. "Tell him to go to hell. I'll call the police."

"No, you can't."

"Why not?" Aaron was confused.

"He had two of his goons with him. One dropped his pants, his cock was hard. He tore off my panties. H..he...he..," she began sobbing again.

"What did the motherfucker do?" He dreaded hearing she may have been raped. He had no idea how he would deal with that if it had happened.

"He pushed his fingers inside me, his nails tore me. The Mayor said if I tell anyone, he will go to the media with my panties and say I came onto him and fucked him." Imogen cried hard.

Aaron gathered her to him and held her tight. *Sonsofbitches, fucking assholes, they are gonna pay for this. They have no idea who they have messed with.*

"I'm so sorry, Aaron."

He held her away from him, placed his fingers under her chin and tilted her head up. "Baby, you have nothing to be sorry about. I'm sorry I wasn't there for you."

"I was so scared. I thought they were going to rape me." She dropped her head back to his now soaked chest.

"Ssssh, it will be okay."

He swept her into his arms and strode to the bedroom. Gently, he lay her down on the bed and undressed her. Once naked, he pulled the covers up to her chin and sat down beside her. "Get some sleep, baby. I'll be right here. We'll stay here for a few days. Fuck the court case." He kissed her lips, pulled the curtains across to plunge the room into darkness, and made his way to the bar for a strong drink. After pouring a whiskey he sat on the lounge and began making calls.

The first was a family friend, the Chief of Police. "Dan, Aaron."

"Aaron, how are you? How's the family?"

"The family is good, but I have a big problem. Can we meet privately?"

"Sounds serious. Where are you?"

"It is, very serious. I'm at the Boulevard."

"I'll be there in fifteen minutes."

Aaron hung up from the call and placed another to the head of security at his company. "Hank?"

"Yes, Boss."

"I need you."

"You at the hotel?"

"Yep. Be here in an hour."

"Will do, Boss."

Hank Lord had been Aaron's Head of Security for almost eight years. He had been involved in some shady operations before they had joined up, but he ran security with military precision. Aaron trusted him completely, he was also a good friend. Hank knew everyone, the good guys and bad. He would deal with their problem quietly and professionally.

***

Aaron checked on Imogen, who now slept quietly. He took a picture of her bruised, beautiful face with his phone to show the Police Chief. He pulled the bedroom door closed as a soft knock at the hotel room door sounded.

"Dan, thanks for coming." Aaron shook the older man's hand and invited him in. "Drink?"

"Just water, on duty."

Aaron padded to the bar and poured the Chief a glass of iced water. They both took a seat.

"What's going on, Aaron?"

"Imogen was threatened and assaulted when she returned to court this afternoon. She's involved in a case where she is prosecuting the Mayor's son for murder."

"Yes, I heard. How the hell did she get threatened and assaulted in a packed courtroom?"

"The courtroom was empty. The Mayor had convinced officials to postpone the trial until tomorrow. Imogen was dragged into a back room."

"By the Mayor?"

"Yep. He slapped her around, her face is badly bruised." He held out the phone with the picture displayed.

Dan studied the image. "Asshole. He bruised her pretty bad. What the fuck did he want?"

"He wanted her to discontinue the trial. He has her panties and said if she told anyone, he would go to the media and say she had come onto him and they fucked. He would show her panties as proof."

Aaron left out the part about the two goons. He would deal with them himself. The Mayor was a different matter, he had to be dealt with legally, or all hell would break loose.

Dan dragged his fingers through his hair. "This fucking Mayor is a pain in the ass. He thinks he is above the law and that bastard son of his is even worse."

"Can you do anything without it becoming too embarrassing for Imogen?"

"Yeah, I think he may have made a mistake. The courthouse has cameras everywhere including the back rooms. Hopefully one was recording. I'll check it out."

Damn, if Dan got his hands on recordings from the back room, he'd find out about the goons. "Dan?"

"Yeah."

"He had a couple of goons with him. It was one of those who tore Imogen's panties off and assaulted her."

Dan stared his friend in the eyes. "You wanted to deal with them? That's why you didn't say anything until I mentioned the cameras."

"Sorry, but one of the bastards finger fucked her. He needs to pay. We won't kill them I promise."

Dan sighed. He was the Chief of Police and he was about to break the law. The reason he would was because he was tired of goons like this being caught by police and set back on the streets by the courts. It was time some of them paid and he was willing to turn a blind eye. *This time.* Maybe it would send a message to some of the other assholes on the streets. "I don't know anything about them, ok? I'll get a copy of the recording sent over to you if there is one."

"Thanks, Dan."

Business completed, the men stood and shook hands and as Aaron opened the door to see Dan out, he found Hank standing on the other side waiting to come in.

"Talk soon, Dan."

Dan glanced at Hank before making his way from the hotel.

"Police Chief? Mixing in important circles, Boss." Hank invited himself in.

"Family friend from way back. I needed him. Scotch and Coke?'

"Thanks."

Hank sat down on the lounge while Aaron fixed their drinks. After handing the scotch and coke to his friend, he joined him.

He explained what had happened to Imogen and answered a couple of Hank's questions.

"Sounds like Barry Jakes and Ron Wild. Evil bastards too. She's lucky she walked away."

"Do you know where to find them?"

"They cover security at a strip joint in Kings Cross, 'Cats and Mice.' Word on the street is, the Mayor has his fingers in the place. Probably why he knows Ron and Barry. I'll head up there tonight and take a couple of pictures, see if Imogen can identify them."

"Thanks, Hank. I knew you would know them."

"Should I be offended or flattered?"

Both men laughed as they finished their drinks. Aaron showed his friend out with a promise from Hank that he would get back to him first thing the next day.

***

It was almost 8pm when hotel room service delivered their dinner. Aaron had ordered crab soup with fresh crusty bread, a chicken salad and Imogen's favorite, Crème Caramel. He hoped it was light enough that she would be able to keep it down. He suspected she was suffering from shock.

He had checked on her several times while she slept. He was concerned by the way she had been tossing and turning. Sweat beaded on her upper lip and forehead, and although the room was cool, she was hot to the touch. If she didn't wake for dinner, he would call the doctor in now.

He padded into the bedroom and switched on a lamp. "Baby, wake up."

Imogen covered her eyes with her arm to prevent the light from hurting. "I'm tired. How long have I been asleep?"

"Almost six hours. You need to wake up and have some dinner."

"Not hungry. I feel sick."

"If you don't sit up and eat, I'll get the doctor. I'm worried, babe." Aaron knew how much Imogen hated doctors and hoped his words would encourage her to sit up, eat and talk to him. It worked.

She sprang up in the bed and settled herself against the pillows. "No doctor please."

Aaron dropped his head guiltily.

"What?"

"A doctor will be up in about an hour to check you."

"No, why?"

"The Police Chief insisted."

"Aaron, I asked you not to tell anyone." Tears streamed over her cheeks. "They will come back for me."

He gathered her into his arms. "Sweetheart, they won't come back. The Chief has had the trial suspended and he has a crew checking the courtroom and adjoining rooms' cameras. We will stay here for a few days until this is cleared up."

"How is it going to be cleared up, Aaron? No-one will believe me over the Mayor, he has my panties remember?"

"Ssssh, let me and Dan worry about that. We won't let him get away with it, I promise."

She tilted her head and studied his eyes. She trusted him with her life, he would never let anything bad happen to her. "Alright. Let's have dinner."

"That's my girl." Aaron placed a kiss to her lips before retrieving the food trolley.

***

Imogen awoke to find Aaron's side of the bed empty. She had slept tucked into the safety of his chest with his arms wrapped around her.

They had talked for a while after the doctor had left. She had prescribed sleeping pills, antibiotics, cream for the tears in her vagina and cream for the gash on her face. As the doctor had described her internal injuries, Aaron had become more and more enraged.

He had lovingly applied the cream and, although his cock had been aroused, he refused to make love to his beautiful lady.

She lay back against the pillows wondering what the time was and where Aaron was. Low voices drifted to her from the lounge room.

Imogen rose from the bed and wrapped herself in a soft, fluffy robe before padding to where the voices were coming from.

"Baby, you're awake." Aaron stood and pulled her into his arms before kissing her thoroughly. "You know Hank, my head of security."

Imogen smiled. "Yes. Hi, Hank."

Aaron pulled her to the couch and onto his lap. "Hank has some photos he would like you to look at."

Imogen was confused. "What of?"

"We think it's the two goons the mayor had with him."

"Oh, no." Imogen's fear was evident, Aaron hugged her close as she buried her head against his chest.

"It's okay. I'm right here. Just a quick glance is all we need. Can you do that for me?"

She swallowed her fear and nodded as she lifted her head. Hank presented an image, she gasped, nodded and tears filled her eyes. When she was shown the second image, the man who had fingered her, she burst into tears. Her body shook as she cried.

Chapter Eight

Aaron carried Imogen to bed and tucked her in. "I need to talk to Hank for a few minutes and I'll be back."

"What are you going to do to those assholes?"

He leaned forward and kissed the tip of her nose. "Don't you worry about it, by the time we're done, they will never bother anyone again. I promise."

Imogen clutched his hand. "Please don't be long."

"I'll be back before you know it." He placed another kiss on her nose, closed the door with a soft click and made his way back to Hank.

"How is she?" Hank inquired when Aaron returned.

"Upset but she'll be fine. I want those pricks taken care of tonight. You are not to kill them. I promised Dan and he can't protect us if you do. Make it so they never hurt anyone else."

"Consider it done, Boss. I will get Jack and Mick to help out. We'll make those bastards pay for what they did to your beautiful lady."

"Tell them a bonus will be coming their way. One for you too. Thanks, Hank."

After seeing Hank out, Aaron padded back to the bedroom, stripped and climbed into bed. Imogen snuggled into his arms before dropping back off to sleep. She had slept a great deal in the past twelve hours, but the doctor had informed him it was normal following trauma.

It was well after lunch when she woke again. Aaron had been lying in bed reading some papers with Imogen draped across his chest. He had endured the most painful of hard-ons all morning but hadn't wanted to disturb her by getting out of bed.

She ran her soft hand over his iron hard cock. "Hmmm, someone is extremely randy."

Aaron placed his papers on the bedside table and hauled her up onto his lap. "Baby, my cock has been at attention all morning with you laying on me. I don't think it will ever return to normal."

Imogen giggled as she kissed each of his nipples in turn.

Aaron groaned. "Have a heart, babe."

She glanced up at him from under her eyelids. She had never looked so sexy. He grew even harder which he hadn't thought possible.

"Guess I will have to set that soldier at ease huh?" Imogen said cheekily.

"You can't yet. You will be sore until at least tomorrow the doc said."

"Since when do we only fuck with a pussy and cock?"

He smiled as realization dawned on him. "Yes please."

She slid down his body, kissing and nipping as she found her way to his now throbbing dick. She lifted him into her hand and slid her tongue along his length. She was so gentle, her touch feather-light. It was agonizing.

"Mmmm, like a lollipop."

"Imogen," he growled.

 She began to sit up. "Had enough?"

"Not fucking likely." He pushed her head back to his cock as she laughed. He loved seeing the mischievous side of her after what she had been through, but not at this moment.

She gently licked across his cum moistened tip and blew gently.

He almost lifted from the bed. He may be her Dom, but she had the power to reduce him to a quivering mess.

"Imogen, please."

She flipped herself onto her back. "Alright, my mouth is all yours, Sir."

Aaron straddled her chest and rammed his cock into her warm, moist, willing mouth. It was heaven. He rocked in and out, her mouth gripped, her tongue slid, teeth nipped, and he erupted like a volcano. The relief was immeasurable. He relaxed and allowed the feeling of euphoria to wash over him.

Imogen kept his satisfied dick firmly lodged in her mouth. She wasn't finished with her master, yet. She smiled at the expression of satisfaction that had taken hold of her lover's face.

She slid her tongue up and down, around and around. His cock flinched as it came back to life. When he attempted to remove it, her lips clamped down hard. A hint of her teeth against his skin let him know she meant business.

"Babe, I need to recover."

She shook her head. *You never let me recover.*

He groaned when she winked at him. He knew if he attempted to move his cock before she was finished, she would bite down and that was one form of sexual play he didn't like. His traitorous cock hardened. He was outnumbered.

The sensation was painfully erotic after being kept hard for so long, finding relief and now enticed to become hard again.

Imogen worked her magic mouth and tongue on Aaron's stiff rod. He thickened and rose under her ministrations. She knew he would be experiencing a mixture of arousal and pain after the trauma his cock had been through with no sex for over sixteen hours.

She had learned, when this had happened in the past, the second orgasm was agonizingly sensational for him. She wanted him to experience that now.

Aaron's body began trembling with painful, but euphoric sensation as his cock rose to the occasion. He had only been in this situation twice before and both times the second orgasm had almost caused him to black out. The bitch remembered. *She will pay when we get home.* The trouble was, they had agreed that only rules Imogen broke at home could be punished.

Her mouth gripped harder, her tongue danced on his cock from every direction while her hands manipulated his balls. He moaned with the intensity of the stimulation. Finally, his orgasm exploded like it had been projected out of a canon. Pain seared down his legs, stars sparkled behind his eyes and he collapsed onto the bed.

Imogen followed as Aaron fell off to one side, keeping his cock firmly in her mouth. Her tongue continued to dance with him as his dick jerked back and forth.

"Imogen, no more. Please."

She smiled up at him and winked. Aaron was begging. Aaron *never* begged. His cock stayed firmly trapped in her cum soaked mouth.

"Please sweetheart. I can't take any more."

She tilted her head to one side.

"No, I am not using the safe word. I will not give in." She had never resorted to the safe word no matter what he had tried, he was damned if he would let her see she was so much stronger than him.

Imogen shrugged and began playing with his hypersensitive penis.

"Let me recover first." *Fuck, I'm gonna pass out.*

She shook her head and began suckling and nipping. He lifted his hands toward her and she glared. Here, in the hotel, the rules were, *he* could not touch her during *her* sexual play just as she couldn't touch him during his. At this time, *he* was hers to do as she wished.

She began kneading and caressing his balls. Pain shot into the back of his head as his cock came to life yet again. *Please, let her stop.* The pressure continued to build until he almost screamed with the agonizing delight. His cock pulsated over and over as he spurted ribbon after ribbon of cum, it seemed he was never going to stop. He groaned in pain.

Imogen released Aaron and began giggling. She had known he was struggling when his cock had refused to stop pulsating and his cum persisted in spurting. She hadn't meant to let go but trying to stifle her giggle had almost caused her to choke. Damn, she had let a good opportunity pass. She was convinced he would have called for safety.

Aaron lay next to her, exhausted. His cock was pulsed on and off. One hand held the base in an attempt to calm the appendage down, the other draped across his sweating forehead.

Imogen tried to creep down and once again capture his throbbing rod. She wasn't quick enough. Aaron grabbed hold of her hair and pulled her back up beside him.

"Enough," he growled.

She hid her face in his chest and giggled.

Even though Aaron was in agony, it delighted him to hear her sweet laughter. He only wished it hadn't been at the expense of his suffering.

***

Hank reported back the following afternoon that the two men had been *taken care of* and wouldn't be bothering anyone else. Aaron didn't ask for details, he trusted his friend to do as he'd asked.

"They won't be walking anywhere for a very long time and sex is now a thing of the past for those assholes."

"Thanks, Hank. Thank Jack and Mick too."

"Will do."

They hung up their phones together.

Aaron went back to watching the film of Imogen's assault. Dan had delivered it personally while she was sleeping, and he had decided to watch it before she awoke.

Imogen awoke and when she found the bed beside her empty, she went in search of Aaron. She wrapped herself in a robe and padded into the lounge room. When she noticed what was on the TV screen, she collapsed to the floor.

"Shit......Imogen."

Aaron threw down the TV control and rushed to her side. He scooped her into his arms and took her back to bed. He patted her hands and gently stroked her face, calling her name. Finally, her eyes fluttered open.

He placed a kiss on her lips. "I'm sorry, babe. I thought you were asleep."

Imogen sat up and he took her into his arms. She was shaking uncontrollably and tears flowed down her cheeks. "It was a shock. I'm okay."

"Hank called. The goons won't be walking for a very long time to come and won't be able to have sex again."

"What does that mean? What did he do to them?"

"I have no idea, didn't ask. Just wanted them fixed, so they don't hurt anyone else."

"Okay."

"Why don't you have a long shower and get dressed? Would you like to go downstairs for dinner?"

"I would like that."

While Imogen showered, Aaron watched the rest of the film. His fists clenched and he shook with anger. *You were so very brave my girl. I am so very proud of you.*

Aaron joined her in the shower and caressed her beautiful body as he soaped her all over. He nipped and suckled at her breasts, slipped a finger tentatively inside her pussy. She flinched and cried out. He pulled back immediately and drew her close.

"I'm sorry, baby. I thought it would be okay by now."

Imogen peered up at him, tears and determination in her eyes. "You caught me by surprise. I am a little tender but not too sore to be fucked. I promise you, when we return from dinner you can have your wicked way with me."

Aaron frowned. Had she flinched and cried out because she had been violated or was it because she was tender. He worried there were residual effects from her attack, and he would need to be very careful with her.

They finished their shower, dressed, and he escorted her to the restaurant. It was wonderful to be free of the room.

***

Dinner had been perfect and Imogen felt so much better. As they undressed for bed, Aaron made the decision to return home the following day. He wanted to get his lady home where she belonged.

"What is happening with the trial?" Imogen asked curiously.

"I'll call Dan and ask. I'll find out how long it's been suspended for." Aaron padded from the room and when Imogen had taken care of her needs and returned to the bedroom, he was waiting for her."

"What did he say?"

"He said it looks like a mistrial. After viewing the tape, the police have charged the Mayor with accessory to murder and for the assault on you. Apparently, he helped his son clean up after he murdered Janet."

Imogen stopped what she was doing. "I don't want my assault to go to court."

"It won't be. They showed him the film from the courthouse camera, and he admitted guilt. Didn't have much choice really with the proof on the television in front of him. He has agreed to give up his son for the murder if they reduce his jail time to ten years. They accepted.”

“So, the trial is over?”

“Looks to be.”

“The mayor wanted it over. Guess he got what he wanted.”

“Yeah, but he copped jail time and got his son imprisoned for a very long time. Not sure that was what he wanted.”

“No, the city is well rid of them both.”

“What will you do now?”

“Not sure. I’ll have to think about it. I do know I’m resigning from the firm and taking a break. I’m not sure if I’ll go back to practicing law.”

The thought of having her all to himself lit up Aaron’s eyes.

Chapter Nine

Aaron turned the key in the lock and stepped inside their apartment.

Imogen followed him in. It was good to be home and she was looking forward to being his Sub again. She had healed well and needed a good fuck.

Aaron slipped straight into Dom mode. "Bedroom."

They had discussed on the way home whether or not her pussy had healed and if she was ready. She was desperate for Aaron to have his cock inside her.

Aaron was relieved to be home. He knew if he needed to be mouth fucked, he was no longer at Imogen's mercy. He couldn't go through another session like the last.

Imogen stripped and dropped to her knees next to the bed. She was dripping with excitement.

Aaron pulled her onto her feet, blindfolded her and lay her onto the bed.

He began caressing her body. "I missed this."

"Me too."

Aaron growled. "You are home Imogen."

Shit, I spoke without permission AND didn't say, Sir.

"Roll over."

She rolled over onto her belly and waited while he bound her legs and arms to the bed. This time he had her spread-eagled. Usually, her hands were together.

She heard drawers opening and closing.

The paddle came down hard and she let out a squeak. Two more slaps came in quick succession and when the fourth one came after a few minutes, the shock caused her to squeak again.

Aaron huffed. But, he would give her some slack, she had been through a great deal.

He ran a brush over her body. The sensation set her nerves on edge and heightened her awareness. She squirmed but refrained from moaning. She had gotten off lightly for her squeals.

The brush danced over the folds of her pussy and wetness began flooding her. She was ready to climax when Aaron stopped. She let out an involuntary groan.

He began untying her hands and feet.

“Did you want to come?”

“Yes.”

“Yes, what?”

“Yes, Sir.”

“You think I’m mean when I stop and you don’t come don’t you?”

“Yes, Sir…..I mean no, Sir. No, Sir.”

Payback time. Aaron grinned as he pulled her to her feet and dragged her onto the deck.

“Please, Sir. Don’t.”

“Did I give permission for you to speak?”

“No, Sir.”

He lay her on the deck chair and secured her hands and feet tightly before gagging her mouth. It wouldn’t do for her to scream and alert their neighbors. He gently slid a butt plug in place before sliding a dildo into her pussy. He turned both on to vibrator mode.

The over stimulation was instant and her first climax burst forth. Within minutes the second erupted followed closely by a third. Imogen bucked violently in the chair causing it to skate over the smooth tiles of the deck. Her screams were muffled as her head thrashed from side to side.

Aaron watched her closely. She had climaxed four times in fifteen minutes. She was becoming distressed. He removed the gag so she could call a stop if she needed to.

"Oh God, I have never felt anything like this before. This is so intense, Aaron."

There was something in her eyes that made him feel wary. Maybe the vibrating butt plug along with the vibrating dildo was more than his girl could handle. It had been worth a try and so far she was doing okay. It was more than could be said for his cock which was iron hard once again. He would pleasure himself inside her once she was done.

Imogen's nipples were bunched, the tightest he had ever seen them. Her body bucked out of control as a huge orgasm slammed into her. Wave after wave seemed to take control of her body. She thrashed, bucked and begged for it to stop. Cum ran like a river between her legs.

"Aaron, stop."

It had been twenty-five minutes, she had tortured him for more than thirty. He was not giving in yet.

"Yellow Rose."

When the words came, barely more than a whisper, Aaron was shocked to his core. He withdrew the butt plug and dildo, unbound her hands and her feet. Imogen was limp, like a ragdoll, as he scooped her into his arms, raced indoors and sat down on the lounge. He felt terrified for the first time in his life. He cradled her to him, rocking back and forth as tears trickled down his cheeks.

"No more, no more," she whispered hoarsely.

"You're safe, baby. No more."

"No. I don't want *this*, *you*, anymore. I want someone to love me. Someone I can hold when I want to and who will hold me when I'm upset. I want to be a Sub part of the time, not all the time. I want a family and a home. I'm done, Aaron." She sobbed against his chest.

Aaron was speechless. He had done the one thing he had been warned never to do – he had broken his Sub. "Baby, you will feel better tomorrow."

"No, I can't stay here. I love you so very much, Aaron, and this life is breaking my heart. I knew the rules when I came, I didn't mean to fall in love with you and I would never ask you to change. You will find someone else." Imogen attempted to stand, but Aaron held her tight.

"Baby, I'm sorry. I can't let you go. I love you too much. We will find a compromise, I promise."

Imogen shook her head. *He loves me?* "I can't ask you to change. It would never work."

Aaron placed her on the lounge and dropped to his knees in front of her. He gathered her hands into his and placed them over his heart. "Imogen Walters, you are the classiest, bravest, most wonderful lady I have ever known. I love you with every fiber of my being. I want...no, I *need* you to agree to become my wife, my lover, my life partner. Please say you'll marry me?"

Imogen thought her ears must be playing tricks on her. "I...I...I don't know what to say."

"Please say yes."

"I love you with all my heart, Aaron, but I can't. It's not what you *really* want. It's not what you need."

"Sweetheart, nothing and I mean *nothing* is more important to me than you. Do I like being your Dom? Shit, yeah. Do I need it all day, every day? Hell, no. Why do you think I take you to the hotel as often as I do?"

Imogen shrugged her shoulders as tears poured down her face.

"It's so I can get away from being a Dom and love you how I know you want to be loved. So you can love me how I want to be loved. I will give away my entire fortune if you'll say yes. Please, baby."

Imogen couldn't believe what was coming out of her lover's mouth. He loved her. *Loved. Her.* "You might need to keep some of our money to provide for Aaron Jnr."

Aaron stared at her confused. "Is that a yes?"

"Aaron Jnr," she ran her hand over her three months pregnant belly, "and I say, yes."

Aaron whooped and swung her into the air before drawing her into his arms and kissing her breathless.

She became worried when he released her and dropped onto the lounge. It was her turn to kneel down before him. "Aaron?" His face was pale and Imogen wondered what was wrong.

"You're pregnant?"

"Yes, we are. Haven't you noticed how easily tears come lately and I have become a little bigger in the tits?"

"I thought the tears were caused by the assault and your tits were bigger....just because. We're pregnant?"

Imogen nodded.

Aaron let out a roar and swung her naked body into the air.

"Aaron, put me down. Look at me. I don't have a stitch on."

Aaron placed her back on the floor and ran his eyes over her gorgeous body. "Please tell me that is one rule that won't change. At least until the baby arrives."

"No, that rule won't change, but some of the others will have to."

"I don't care. How about we make our hotel visits Dom and Sub time? We don't go very often, but it will be often enough to satisfy both our urges."

"I think it's a great idea." She pulled him down for a kiss.

"From tonight, we are equals in this apartment. We can touch when we want to, argue, hell, whatever you want. I'm gonna be a daddy!"

Imogen burst into tears and began laughing. She had never been so happy.

He gathered her into his arms and peppered her face with kisses. "I love you so much. .....Mine."

About the Author

I'm an Australian author who writes in a variety of genres, including Western romance, historical romance, Gay Romance, and contemporary romance.

I have published over 60 books and novellas, many of which feature strong, independent heroines and rugged, alpha male heroes. Some of my popular series include the Outback Australia series and The Carter Brothers series.

My books are known for their well-researched historical details and vivid descriptions of the Australian landscape.

My work has garnered praise from readers and critics alike, and I have won several awards for my writing.

If you're interested in learning more about my books:
Linktree
https://linktr.ee/SusanHorsnell

For Australian Historical Romance written under Annabel Vaughan
https://linktr.ee/annabelvaughan